All the Colors of the Earth

SHEILA HAMANAKA

MORROW JUNIOR BOOKS   NEW YORK

Oil paints on canvas were used for the full-color illustrations.
The text type is 22-point Hiroshige Medium.

Copyright © 1994 by Sheila Hamanaka

7   8   9   10

Library of Congress Cataloging-in-Publication Data
Hamanaka, Sheila. All the colors of the Earth / Sheila Hamanaka.   p.   cm.
Summary: Reveals in verse that despite outward differences children everywhere are essentially
the same and all are lovable.
ISBN 0-688-11131-9 (trade)—ISBN 0-688-11132-7 (library)
[1. Brotherliness—Fiction.   2. Stories in rhyme.]   I. Title.   PZ8.3.H17A1 1994
[E]—dc20   93-27118   CIP   AC

To Suzy and Kiyo and all the other children of the earth

Children come in all the colors of the earth—

The roaring browns of bears and soaring eagles,

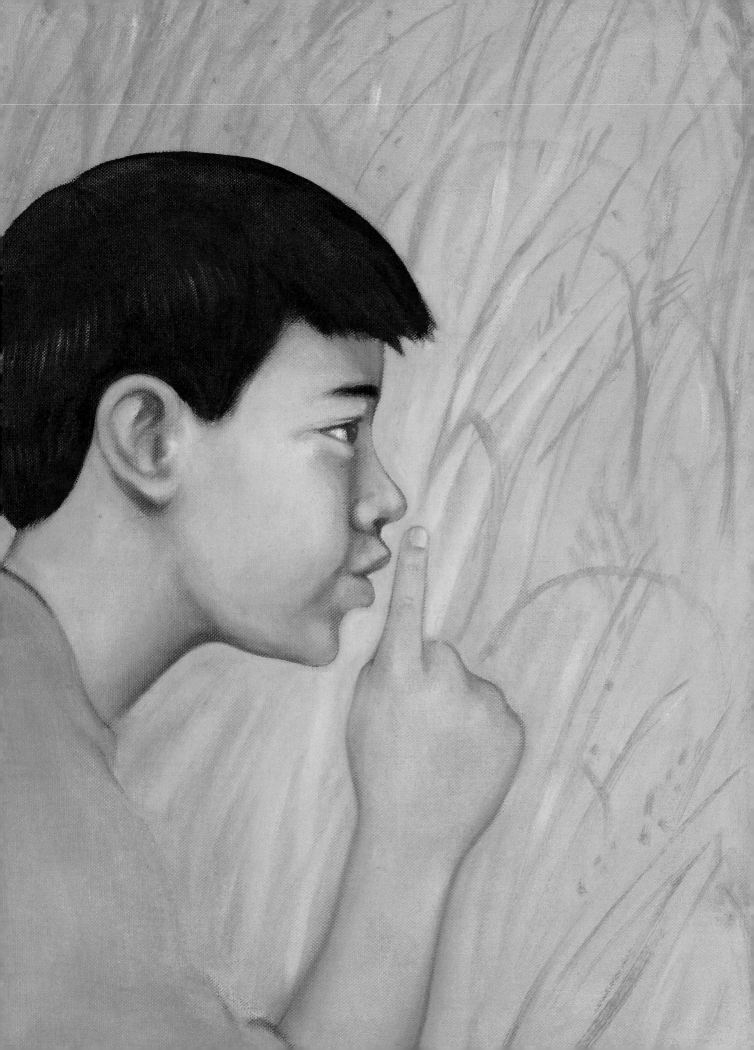

The whispering golds of late summer grasses,

And crackling russets of fallen leaves,

The tinkling pinks of tiny seashells
by the rumbling sea.

Children come with hair like bouncy baby lambs,

Or hair that flows like water,

Or hair that curls like sleeping cats in snoozy cat colors.

Children come in all the colors of love,

In endless shades of you and me.

For love comes in cinnamon,
walnut, and wheat,

Love is amber and ivory and ginger and sweet

Like caramel, and chocolate, and the honey of bees.

Dark as leopard spots, light as sand,

Children buzz with laughter that kisses our land,

With sunlight like butterflies happy and free,

Children come in all the colors
of the earth and sky and sea.